SO MUCH SNOW!

Robert Munsch

illustrated by
Michael Martchenko

Scholastic Canada Ltd.
New York Toronto London Auckland Sydney
Mexico City New Delhi Hong Kong Buenos Aires

Scholastic Canada Ltd.
604 King Street West, Toronto, Ontario M5V 1E1, Canada

Scholastic Inc.
557 Broadway, New York, NY 10012, USA

Scholastic Australia Pty Limited
PO Box 579, Gosford, NSW 2250, Australia

Scholastic New Zealand Limited
Private Bag 94407, Botany, Manukau 2163, New Zealand

Scholastic Children's Books
Euston House, 24 Eversholt Street, London NW1 1DB, UK

www.scholastic.ca

The art for this book was painted in watercolour on Crescent illustration board.
The type is set in 21 point Barcelona ITC Std.

Library and Archives Canada Cataloguing in Publication

Munsch, Robert N., 1945-, author
So much snow! / Robert Munsch ; illustrated by Michael Martchenko.

ISBN 978-1-4431-4617-3 (paperback)

I. Martchenko, Michael, illustrator II. Title.

PS8576.U575S58 2016b jC813'.54 C2016-902571-3

8 7 6 5 4 Printed in Canada 119 17 18 19 20 21

For Jasmine Moran,
Lockport, New York.
— R.M.

"A blizzard! A blizzard! A blizzard!" said Jasmine's mother. "Maybe you should not go to school today."

"There is no snow *now*," said Jasmine. "And besides, I like snow. I want to go to school. It's Pizza Day."

"Dress really warm," said her mother.

So Jasmine dressed really warm. Right away, it started to snow very hard.

Jasmine sang:

"Neat! Neat! Snowy feet!
Snowy feet can't be beat.
Neat! Neat! Snowy feet!
Snowy feet can't be beat.
Wintertime is fun!"

Jasmine walked down the road toward the school. By the time she got to the corner, the snow was up to her knees.

Jasmine sang:

"Gee! Gee! Frozen knees!
Boots are filling up on me.
Gee! Gee! Frozen knees!
Boots are filling up on me.
Wintertime is fun!"

Jasmine walked and walked and walked, and soon the snow was up to her bum.

Jasmine sang:

"Poor bum! Frozen numb!
Snow's so deep, I can't run.
Poor bum! Frozen numb!
Snow's so deep, I can't run.
Wintertime is fun."

Jasmine walked and walked and walked. She could see the school, but the snow was up to her nose.

Jasmine sang:

“Oh no, it’s at my nose!
What if the whole world froze?
Oh no, it’s at my nose!
What if the whole world froze?
Wintertime is fun?”

Jasmine stopped walking and the snow kept coming down and soon only the top of her hat was above the snow.

Jasmine sang:

"Oh, dread! Over my head!
I wish I was home in bed!
Oh, dread! Over my head!
I wish I was home in bed!
Wintertime's no fun."

She stood there singing for a long time. Finally the school caretaker came stomping through the snow on a pair of snowshoes.

He pulled up Jasmine by her hat and yelled, "AHHHHHHHHHHH! Frozen kid!"

Then he went stomping back through the blizzard, pulling Jasmine behind him.

"Where are we going?" said Jasmine.

"I'm taking you to the nurse's office," said the caretaker. "We will get you warmed up and if you are OK, I will take you to your classroom."

So he took Jasmine inside to the nurse's office and dropped her onto a chair.

The vice principal came in and said, "You're frozen stiff! Let's get you warmed up. Here are some nice blankets."

She wrapped Jasmine in ten layers of blankets, but Jasmine did not unfreeze.

The school secretary came in and said, "You're frozen stiff! Let's get you warmed up. I will go get you a nice cup of hot chocolate."

She poured the hot chocolate into Jasmine's mouth.

"Yum!" said Jasmine, but she did not unfreeze.

Finally the caretaker came back. He took one look at Jasmine and said, "You're still frozen? Let me see what I can do."

He got a huge duster and tickled Jasmine under the chin.

Jasmine started to laugh and

the ice shattered into a million pieces.

So the caretaker took her to
her class. On the way there they
went past the principal's office.

"Hey," said the principal, "what are you two doing here? There's a blizzard outside and it is not going to stop, so we are having a snow day! Everyone has to go home!"

"Wait a minute!" said Jasmine. "It's Pizza Day!"

So they all went out for lunch and Jasmine sang: